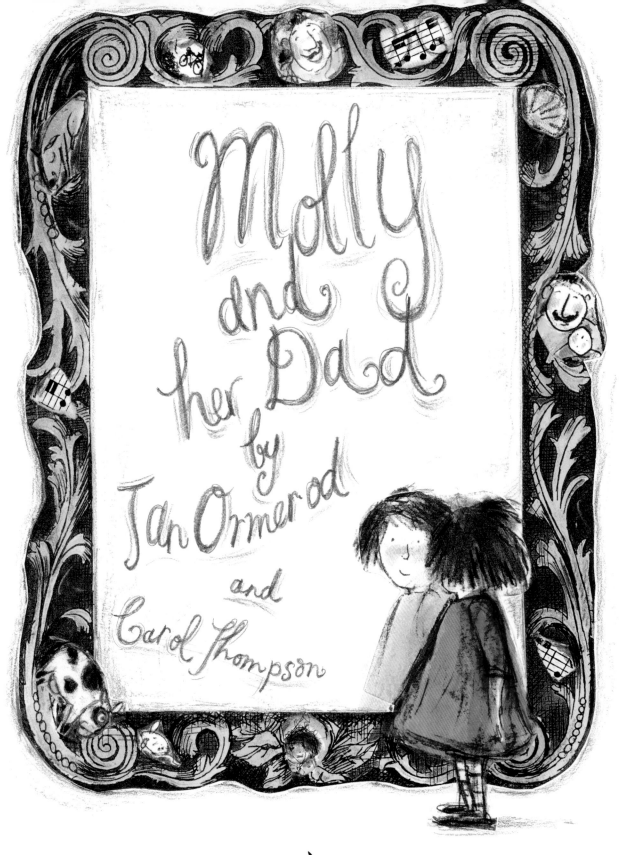

Molly and her Dad

by

Jan Ormerod

and

Carol Thompson

LITTLE HARE
www.littleharebooks.com

Little Hare Books
8/21 Mary Street, Surry Hills
NSW 2010 AUSTRALIA

www.littleharebooks.com

First published in the USA in 2008 by Roaring Brook Press
First published in Australia in 2008
First published in paperback in 2009

National Library of Australia
Cataloguing-in-Publication entry

Ormerod, Jan. 1946-

Molly and her dad / author, Jan Ormerod ; illustrator, Carol Thompson.

Surry Hills, N.S.W. : Little Hare Books, 2009.

ISBN: 978 1 921272 97 4 (pbk.)

For primary school age.

Fathers and daughters--Juvenile fiction.
Family reunions--Juvenile fiction.

Thompson, Carol.

A823.4

Designed by Roaring Brook Press
Additional design by Bernadette Gethings
Produced by Pica Digital, Singapore
Printed in China through Phoenix Offset

5 4 3 2 1

For Angela
—J. O.

For Jenny
—C. T.

Molly loves to tell stories, especially stories about her dad, who lives a whole plane ride away.

Molly's mother says
she looks just like her dad,
but when Molly looks
at photos of him
she thinks . . .

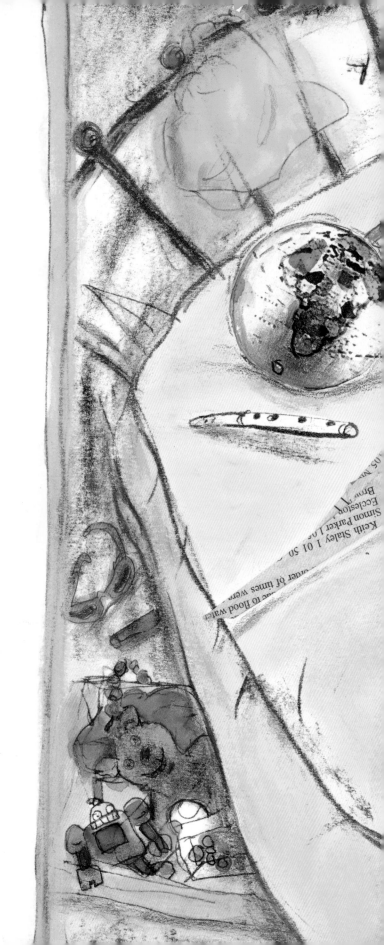

At school, other children's dads come to visit Molly's class.

Leo's papa grows things.

Maria's daddy brings them lots of paper to draw on.

Jasmine's pa can balance on a tightrope.

Woody's dad is a builder.

Molly tells her class, "My mum is going away for a week, and my daddy is coming to look after me—and it is not a story, it is really true!"

Then,
KNOCK, KNOCK!
DING, DONG!
It's Molly's dad and
he is big and noisy.
He smiles a big smile
and laughs a loud laugh.

Molly's dad cooks pizzas that taste funny.

He sings silly songs and
dances around the house.

Molly doesn't know
what name to call him—
Father, Papa, Daddy, Joe?
She doesn't call him anything.

The first morning, they both wake up late.
Then it was all rush and muddle.

wheeeeee

Molly takes her dad into school to meet her class,
and he tells them wonderful stories.

He tells them a scary story,

a sad story,

and a silly story about a cow and a dog.

And Molly is proud of her dad.

After school, they go shopping together and choose
smelly cheese and crusty bread and big bottles
of fizzy apple juice to share, and Dad buys
face paints just for Molly.
And now Molly knows just what to call him—
she calls him Dad.

They cook pizzas together, not too spicy,
and Dad calls her Molly.
They hang Christmas lights and
Molly puts on her party dress.

That night, they play loud music and dance
till the little house bounces, and the neighbours join in.

Later, Dad tells her stories
about when she was
a baby girl, until her
eyes close and she
drifts into sleep.

Now Mum is back home,

and it's time to say goodbye.

And now, when Molly says
"my dad" at school, they know
just what he is like—and so does
Molly. He is just like her.